Pidge
TAKES THE STAGE

WRITTEN & CREATED BY
MICHELLE STAUBACH GRIMES

ILLUSTRATED BY
BILL DEORE

Pidge Media LLC | whereispidge.com

Names: Grimes, Michelle Staubach, author. | DeOre, Bill, illustrator.
Title: PIDGE TAKES THE STAGE / Michelle Staubach Grimes ; illustrated by Bill DeOre.
Description: Dallas, TX: Pidge Media, LLC, 2018.
Identifiers: ISBN 978-0-9908420-1-9 | LCCN 2017959443
Summary : Pidge and her canine buddy Maverick audition for the school musical. Pidge learns that unconditional love matters more than fame.
Subjects: LCSH Singing--Juvenile fiction. | Dogs--Juvenile fiction. | Dog training--Juvenile fiction. | Children's plays--Juvenile fiction. | BISAC JUVENILE FICTION / General | JUVENILE FICTION / Animals.
Classification: LCC PZ7.G884285 Pi 2018 | DDC [E]—dc23

The illustrations in this book are rendered in pencil, pen, ink and watercolor. Typography/font Poster Bodoni BT and Oxtail OT

10 9 8 7 6 5 4 3 2 1
Printed in Canada. First Printing, February 2018.

Design by Pixel Mouse House

To my siblings – Jennifer, Stephanie, Jeff, and Amy,

Thank you for loving me through both the good and hard times. Our sibling bond is unbreakable. I'm thankful for each of you.

Love,
Michelle

Pidge couldn't wait to share her big news.
"Mav and I are auditioning for the school musical!"
she said.

"You can't sing," said Drew. "And a real dog?"

"I can learn! And yes, they want a real dog."

"But Mav doesn't behave," said Katrina.

"Yeah, look," said Cody, as Mav helped
himself to breakfast.

"Sit, Mav." Pidge had to push Maverick down until they both collapsed on the floor.

"He might not be ready," Dad said.

"He's gonna get ready," said Pidge. "And so am I!"

But Pidge knew they needed help.
"Mrs. Jackson, will you give me voice lessons for the school musical?"
Pidge asked her friend Billy's mom.

"Of course," Mrs. Jackson said.
"But it takes a lot of unspectacular preparation
to get spectacular results. Are you up for that?"

"I'm ready!" Pidge said. "And Mav is auditioning too.
Billy, will you help me train him?"
"Dude, you're nuts. Mav can't be trained."
Pidge gave him a look.
"Of course I will," said Billy.

The next day, the official training began.

"Come here, boy," Pidge said. Mav came. Well, kind of.
"Sit!" Pidge commanded. Maverick didn't.
"Try a treat," Billy said.

"And, let's try fetching."
Mav's never fetched anything except food off the table,
thought Pidge. Maybe her family was right.
Maybe Mav couldn't be trained.

The following morning Pidge had her
first voice lesson.

"Stand up straight and repeat after me,"
said Mrs. Jackson.

"Ahhhh," sang Pidge.

"Focus on your breath," Mrs. Jackson said while
picking out notes on the piano.

Pidge did.

"OK, let's try scales," said Mrs. Jackson.
"Do, Re, Mi, Fa, So."

Pidge copied her, kind of.

"Okay, a little more now. Do, Re, Mi, Fa, So, La, Ti, Do."

Pidge took a deep breath.
"Do, Re, Mi, Ti, Darn. Do, Re, Ti. This is so hard!"

"It's okay. Let's work on opening your throat now."

Pidge stretched her mouth so wide it hurt. Tears welled in her eyes.
What have I gotten myself into? She thought.

At home,
Pidge practiced
in front of the mirror.

"Mav, you gotta practice too.
We only have a few more days,"
Pidge said.

Pidge's practice paid off!

But things weren't going quite so well with Maverick.

"Mav, listen!" Billy commanded.

"You must come through for Pidge. Now shake."

Mav shook – a dirty sock.

On audition day, Pidge's whole family
– and Billy – cheered her on.

Pidge tugged Maverick up the school steps.

When it was Maverick's turn, the judge said,
    "We need to be sure you respond to commands, ok, pup?
        Now sit."

Maverick leaped off the stage and
raced up the aisle, whacking kids
as he passed.

"Ouch!" they yelled.

"Stop!" the judge demanded.

Pidge tumbled off the stage,
but before she could catch him,
Maverick had a bag of chips
in his mouth.

Pidge ran faster.

Still out of reach, Maverick got caught on Mrs. Lewis' skirt. The whole world could see her slip!

Everyone roared with laughter, except Mrs. Lewis.

Pidge and Maverick landed on the floor in the middle of a heavy pile of stage curtains.

"I hope you're more prepared than that dog," the judge said.

Billy took Maverick by the collar and whispered to Pidge,
"I've got Mav. You sing."

Pidge stood up straight and took
a deep breath. Her voice cracked.
She took another breath.
And then?
She sang!

The next day, the cast list was posted.

"Bummer, I didn't get the lead. I'm playing the middle child – just like at home!" said Pidge.

"Awwwww, Pidge. Every role is important," Billy said.

"That's what Mom and Dad always say," laughed Pidge. "Maybe I'll get the lead NEXT time."

"I bet you will."

"Hey Billy – was I silly to make Mav audition?" Pidge asked.

"No, but it's silly to think he'd ever be anything but good ol' Mav," Billy said. "Annnndddd.......it looks like HE'S got the lead right now."

"**STOPPPPP!**...." Pidge yelled. "Not the creek."

"We're always in the MIDDLE..." Pidge said, "of a MESS."

"I'd rather be in the middle of a mess with you and Mav than anywhere else," Billy said.